# Fancy NANCY

## Stellar Stargazer!

BY THE #1 *NEW YORK TIMES* BESTSELLING AUTHOR AND ILLUSTRATOR DUO

Jane O'Connor and Robin Preiss Glasser

**HARPER**

*An Imprint of HarperCollinsPublishers*

For Judy Donnelly, who is stellar in countless ways!
—J. O'C.

For Heaven—a little one whose time on Earth will always be cherished
—R.P.G.

This book has been checked by Summer Ash, research associate at the
Hayden Planetarium Division of Physical Sciences, Department of
Astrophysics. Happy stargazing!

Fancy Nancy: Stellar Stargazer!
Text copyright © 2011 by Jane O'Connor
Illustrations copyright © 2011 by Robin Preiss Glasser
All rights reserved. Printed in the United States of America.
No part of this book may be used or reproduced in any manner whatsoever without written permission
except in the case of brief quotations embodied in critical articles and reviews. For information address
HarperCollins Children's Books, a division of HarperCollins Publishers,
10 East 53rd Street, New York, NY 10022.
www.harpercollinschildrens.com

Library of Congress Cataloging-in-Publication Data is available.
ISBN 978-0-06-191523-9

Typography by Jeanne L. Hogle
11  12  13  14  15    LPR    10  9  8  7  6  5  4  3  2  1
❖
First Edition

GREETINGS AND SALUTATIONS,

## fellow earthlings!

That's fancy for "Hi, everybody here
on good old planet Earth!"

Is anything more magnificent than a dark sky filled
with twinkling, shimmering, glittering stars? My dad
and I both love to stargaze. (Gazing is way fancier than
just looking at something.)

And tonight, for the very first time,
I will get to sleep outside under the stars.
Keep your fingers crossed that
it's a clear night!

Love,
Nancy

We are eating alfresco (that's fancy for outside) and waiting for the sky to grow dark.

My little sister is so impatient! She keeps tugging on my arm and asking, "Where are the stars? I want stars!"

Starlight Motel

So I tell JoJo, "A star is out right now." She thinks I'm teasing, but I'm not. Because guess what . . .

The sun is a star. It's much closer than any other star. That's why it looks so big. During the day, its bright light blocks out all the other stars. The other stars are always up there in the sky—we just can't see them until the sun sets and the sky is dark.

"Can you wish on the sun?" JoJo asks.

Hmmmm … It is a star, after all. So why not! We close our eyes and say, "Star light, star bright, first star I see tonight. I wish I may, I wish I might, have this wish I wish tonight."

STELLAR SECRET:
I wished for something extra special to appear in the sky.

Warning to all Stargazers: Never, ever look right at the sun, even if you're wearing glamorous sunglasses or using binoculars.

It will damage—that is fancy for hurt—your eyes.

Now JoJo sees the moon, and she wants to wish on that, too. "No, you can't," I tell her. "That's definitely against the rules because the moon isn't a star."

"But it's shining," JoJo says.

So I draw a picture for her to help her understand.

"The moon is made of rock. It can't shine on its own. Light from the sun reflecting off the moon makes it look like it's shining. Understand?"

Guess what! You could lie under the moon for hours and hours and never get a moon burn.

"Hey," I say to my sister, "want to pretend we are astronauts going to the moon?"

We go get our space suits, and soon we are ready to blast off.

STELLAR FACT:

It takes three whole days for a spaceship to reach the moon.

Now we count down—10, 9, 8, 7, 6, 5, 4, 3, 2, 1—BLASTOFF!

When we land, we breathe through our tanks because there is no air on the moon. On the moon it is boiling hot during the day and freezing cold at night—there's no in-between. But our space suits protect us.

TurboJet Vac

We go exploring. All we see are rocks and dust. Everything is gray or brown, which are my least favorite colors. "Isn't it dreary?" I say to astronaut JoJo. (Dreary is fancy for dark and ugly.)

So is anything fun on the moon?
Turn the page to find out!

Yes! On the moon you don't walk, you bounce—it's like being on a trampoline!

Boing!

Boing!

Boing!

CLANCY
1

Spaceships don't have ovens, so we can't cook. No problem! I brought along a bag of real astronaut ice cream that I bought on a class trip to the planetarium. Real astronauts eat this stuff. We pour on some chocolate sauce and—voilà!—it's an outer-space sundae.

We plant a flag just like the first men on the moon did. Their flag is still there.

Astronaut JoJo and I drive a lunar vehicle (that's fancy for moon car) back to our spaceship. We are ready to return home.

"Greetings and salutations, fellow earthlings!"
I say when we land.

"Welcome back. See any aliens?" my dad asks.

My dad is teasing. There are no aliens
(that's fancy for space creatures).

When the moon is full, you can sort of see a face—that's
why people say there's a man in the moon.
   Here is my drawing. I made the man in the moon a
lady—a *très* fancy lady!

Because of the way the sun shines on the moon, it looks different every night. Tonight it looks like a skinny banana. That's called a crescent moon. Every night the moon appears a little bigger until it's a full moon. Then it starts shrinking all the way back down to a crescent moon again.

Ooh la la! A few stars are out.

They really do look like diamonds in the sky, just like it says in "Twinkle, Twinkle, Little Star." Right away I locate—that's fancy for find—the North Star.

Long ago, sailors could tell which way their ship was going by looking for the North Star. Finding your way by starlight sounds so romantic!

My dad and I try to locate some constellations. They are groups of stars that make a picture like a connect-the-dots puzzle. There are bears and dogs, swans and whales. I love the legends—that's a fancy word for stories—about constellations.

The easiest constellation to find is the Big Dipper.
A dipper is like a big spoon.

One of the most famous constellations is called the Hunter.
The Hunter's name is Orion—you say it like this: oh-ry-un.
He can be seen in the cold months. He was handsome and brave,
but he bragged all the time.

We are having trouble finding any constellations because—uh-oh!—big clouds are moving across the sky.

"It will probably clear up," Dad says, and while we wait I make up my own constellation—I call it the Diamond Tiara.

I tell my dad, "Long ago, a beautiful princess named Nanette fell in love with a commoner. (I explain to him that's a fancy word for someone who isn't royal.)

## THE LEGEND OF THE DIAMOND TIARA

The king wouldn't let Nanette marry him. One day she ran away.

She wore plain, ugly clothes so she wouldn't look like a princess.

Only she forgot one thing—she still had on her diamond tiara.

The palace guards nearly caught her.

The second Nanette got outside, she took off her tiara and threw it

up, up, up into the sky, where it joined the other stars."

The End

"That's a wonderful legend," my dad says. "Did she find the commoner and get married?"

"*Mais oui!*" All my stories have happy endings.

It is very cloudy and windy now. My mom takes
JoJo inside, but I am determined to camp out overnight.
Determined means I'm sticking it out no matter what.
My dad makes a fire and we roast marshmallows.

Starlight
Motel

It is cozy in my sleeping bag. I hear raindrops plip-plopping on our tent. My dad says, "It wasn't a stellar night for stars, but we had fun."

The next thing I know, it's morning and Dad wakes me up, shouting, "Quick! Come look!"

Ooh la la! My wish came true. Something extra special is in the sky.

I think rainbows are just as magnificent as stars. Don't you?